My Very First Winnie the Pooh™

Pooh's
First Day of School

Written by
Kathleen W. Zoehfeld

Illustrated by
Robbin Cuddy

SCHOLASTIC INC.

New York Toronto London Auckland Sydney
Mexico City New Delhi Hong Kong Buenos Aires

First published by Disney Press, New York, NY.
This edition published by Scholastic Inc., 90 Old Sherman Turnpike, Danbury, CT 06816
by arrangement with Disney Licensed Publishing.

SCHOLASTIC and associated logos are trademarks
and/or registered trademarks of Scholastic Inc.

ISBN 0-7172-8869-2

Printed in the U.S.A.

"School is starting! School is starting!" cried Tigger. "Come on! Don't be late!"

"School?" asked Winnie the Pooh. "What are you talking about?"

"Christopher Robin has a new backpack and lunch box, and he's getting ready for school. We better get ready, too!"

"Oh, Tigger," said Pooh. "School is for children. Not for fluff and stuffing like us."

"What do you mean, not for us?" asked Tigger. "Tiggers LOVE to go to school."

"Piglets don't love school," said Piglet thoughtfully. "At least I don't think we do."

"You're right, Piglet," said Eeyore. "This schooling business—pencils and whatnot—it's overrated if you ask me."

"I think it sounds great!" cried little Roo. "Can I go, too?"

"Come along, Roo," said Pooh. "We'll all go see Christopher Robin. Maybe he can tell us more about it."

Tigger was the first to bound through Christopher Robin's door. "OK, where's the school?" he asked.

"It's about a mile away," said Christopher Robin. "The school bus will come tomorrow morning to take me there."

"A mile?" asked Piglet, pulling his ear.

"**I**t's not here in the Hundred-Acre Wood?" asked Tigger.

"If you have to go that far from home, I'm sure school is not a good thing for Piglets," said Piglet.

"We don't have the brains for it anyway," said Pooh.

"You'd all like school," said Christopher Robin. "I'm sure you would. Wait right here a minute, and I'll make a classroom just for us."

"Imagine, our very own school!" said Pooh. "I wonder if we're up to it."

"Can we bounce in school?" asked Roo.

"Of course you can, little buddy!" said Tigger. "School's the bounciest place there is!"

"There's no bouncing in school," said Eeyore decisively.

"None?" asked Tigger.

"School is work. No time for fun," said Eeyore.

"Not even a little?" asked Tigger. His shoulders drooped.

Eeyore shook his head knowingly.

"Oh," said Tigger, in a very small voice for a Tigger. "Maybe Tiggers don't like school after all."

He and Piglet were about to tiptoe away when Christopher Robin called out, "Time for school to begin!"

"Oh d-dear," said Piglet.

Christopher Robin set up a table, and around it he put chairs, just the right size for Poohs and Piglets.

"We always sing a song first," said Christopher Robin as they gathered around. *"Good morning to Tigger, good morning to Roo. Welcome, all children, good morning to you. . . .* Now everyone join in!"

"This is fun, Piglet. Don't you think?" whispered Pooh.

"Shhh," said Piglet.

"Good morning," they all sang.

"If it is a good morning," said Eeyore, "which I doubt."

"Well, the first morning at school can be hard," said Christopher Robin. "But I've met my new teacher, and I know she's really nice. And I know two friends who will be in my class."

"It *is* friendly to spend your days with friends," said Piglet.

"And we learn things in school, too," said Christopher Robin.

"That may be OK for you," said Pooh. "But we're nothing but stuffing. Do you really think a little schooling will improve us?"

"Sure," said Christopher Robin. "You can learn to write your ABCs. It's fun."

Christopher Robin handed out paper and crayons. "Let's all draw pictures of ourselves."

"What does that have to do with ABCs?" asked Tigger.

"The best letters of the alphabet are the letters in our own names," said Christopher Robin. "When our pictures are finished, we can write our names on them."

Pooh chewed the end of his purple crayon. "P-O-O-H," he printed slowly.

"Very nice!" cried Christopher Robin.

"P-T," tried Piglet, whose name was really quite complicated.

Eeyore, who only knew the letter A, wrote it under his picture. "Don't know when I've had so much fun," he said proudly.

Roo made some quotation marks.

Tigger made a squiggle.

Everyone did a fine job.

"Counting is easy, too," said Christopher Robin. "Pooh, let's see how high you can stack these blocks."

"1, 2, 3, 4, 5, 6," Pooh counted.

It was turning into a lovely tower. But when Tiggers see towers, they think, "Towers are for bouncing," and . . .

CRASH! Down went the blocks.

"Oh," sighed Pooh.

"Tig-ger!" said Christopher Robin sternly.

"Sorry," said Tigger. "All these ABCs and 1-2-3s are fine, but what about fun? What good is a place if you can't even bounce in it?"

"It's true, you can't bounce when your teacher is talking," said Christopher Robin, "but my school has a playground, and we get to go outside and play nearly every day."

"A real playground?" asked Roo.

"Yes," said Christopher Robin. "A real playground with slides and swings and everything."

"I knew Tiggers loved school!" cried Tigger.

But Pooh, whose tummy was beginning to feel a bit rumbly, was worried about something else.

"I hope you're allowed to eat at school," he said.

"Oh yes," said Christopher Robin. "That's what my new lunch box is for. I'm going to bring a peanut-butter-and-honey sandwich, a banana, and milk."

"*Mmmm*," sighed Pooh wistfully.

And then Christopher Robin, who knew his friend very well, said, "Why don't we have a little snack right now?"

He set out a large pot of honey, and everyone had a lick.

"Christopher Robin, I hope your new teacher is as nice as you are," said Piglet.

"Yes!" agreed Pooh. "Can we play again tomorrow?"

"PLEASE?!" cried all the rest.

"Of course," said Christopher Robin. "We'll play every day—as soon as I'm home from school."